For Libba Moore Gray

A. B.

For Tom, Lois, Isabel, and Joe

C. M.

SIMON & SCHUSTER BOOKS FOR YOUNG READERS
Simon & Schuster Building
Rockefeller Center
1230 Avenue of the Americas
New York, New York 10020
Text copyright © 1993 by Alan Benjamin
Illustrations copyright © 1993 by Carol Morley
Originally published in Great Britain by ABC, All Books for
Children, a division of The All Children's Company Ltd.
First U.S. edition 1994
SIMON & SCHUSTER BOOKS FOR YOUNG READERS is a trademark of Simon & Schuster.
Manufactured in Singapore
10 9 8 7 6 5 4 3 2 1
Library of Congress Cataloging-in-Publication Data
is available upon request.
Library of Congress Catalog Card Number is 93-31161.
ISBN 0-671-88718-1

Buck

Written by Alan Benjamin

Illustrated by Carol Morley

SIMON & SCHUSTER BOOKS FOR YOUNG READERS
Published by Simon & Schuster
New York London Toronto Sydney Tokyo Singapore

My old dog, Buck,
was not the same.
The years had made him
slow and lame.

I traded Buck
to Farmer Ben
for one fine rooster,
one fat hen.

My house grew full
of eggs until
I swapped them for
a whippoorwill.

Her song, though lovely,
spoiled my rest.
I swapped her for
an oaken chest.

The chest was full
of keys, and these
I traded for
a hive of bees.

They made more honey
than I could keep.

I swapped them for
a woolly sheep.

Then when she filled
my house with wool,
I swapped her for
a Brahman bull.

He bucked and bellowed
night and day.
I swapped him for
a Chevrolet.

The day its tires
needed air,
I swapped it for
a racing mare.

She won the derby,
and I made

a fortune from

that lucky trade.

Then I was rich
and bought some land,
and built myself
a palace grand.

But through its rooms
of silk and stone,
I wandered sadly
all alone.

I swapped it all
with Farmer Ben
to have my old Buck
back again.

My faithful friend
is slow and lame,
but life without him's
not the same.